Ever After High®

DRAGON GAMES

Welcome, Baby Dragons!

Adapted by Margaret Green

Based on the screenplay by Sherry Klein, Shadi Petosky, Keith Wagner, MJ Offen, and Audu Paden

LITTLE BROWN & COMPANY
LB kids

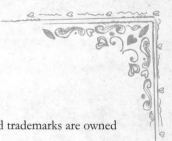

Little, Brown and Company

Hachette Book Group
1290 Avenue of the Americas, New York, NY 10104
Visit us at lb-kids.com

Little, Brown and Company is a division of Hachette Book Group, Inc.
The Little, Brown name and logo are trademarks of Hachette Book Group, Inc.

The publisher is not responsible for websites (or their content) that are not owned by the publisher.

First Edition: February 2016

ISBN 978-0-316-30179-4
LCCN: 2015951635

10 9 8 7 6 5 4 3 2 1

CW

Printed in the United States of America

Of all the pets at Ever After High, Nevermore was the best, in Raven Queen's eyes. She felt lucky to have the dragon as her pet. Nevermore was always looking out for Raven—like the time she leapt in front of the Evil Queen's mirror so that Raven wouldn't accidentally shatter it and let her mother out.

"AAAUGH, Nevermore!" shrieked the Evil Queen.

Nevermore shrank in fear and scampered away to hide in a pile of paint cans.

Raven picked up her paint-covered pet. "Nice try, Mom, but you're not getting out that easily."

When Raven climbed down from the tower
and returned to her locker, Nevermore's colorful
appearance attracted some attention.

"What happened to you?" asked Holly O'Hair.

Her twin sister, Poppy, petted the dragon and
looked up at Raven. "Someone sure needs a bath!"

"My mom really spooked Nevermore,"
explained Raven. "She wound up with a bit of
a messy makeover."

"We can groom Nevermore for you," offered Holly.

"Sounds like the perfect job for us!" Poppy added.

But the O'Hair twins soon discovered that taking care of a dragon wasn't easy! One minute Nevermore was calmly letting the girls wash the paint off her scales, and the next minute she got spooked and went flying all over the stables, making a giant mess.

"Poppy, we're going to need some kind of armor if we're going to stay in the dragon-grooming business," said Holly.

The next time Holly and Poppy groomed Nevermore, they were prepared with all the armor they could find. They were still no match for the nervous dragon, though. They tried out a new scale polish on her and a terrified Nevermore flew away!

The twins rushed back to the castle to tell Raven. "We're sorry!" they said. "Maybe if you call her, she'll come back."

"Thanks for getting me," said Raven. "Let's go!"

As the girls walked around the grounds
looking for Nevermore, they came across the
old Dragon Games arena.

"Why did Headmaster Grimm close the
Dragon Center down?" asked Apple White.

"You mean, you don't know?" asked Holly.
She pulled up a video on her MirrorPad.

"Dragon Games can be *very* dangerous," she explained. "They say that Snow White and the Evil Queen were the greatest Dragon Games captains ever after! They were wicked competitive."

Just then, a dragon cry rang through the air. The girls raced into the old dragon stables.

When they walked into the stables, Nevermore immediately popped out of a bale of hay and ran to Raven's side. But it wasn't Raven's dragon who had made the cry.

It was Daring Charming's favorite dragon, Legend. Poppy and Holly raced over to the moaning creature.

"Please help him," Daring cried.

"Body temperature is really high!" said Holly. "I think it's time."

Legend was laying dragon eggs! Daring's favorite dragon was a girl!

"Dragonpedia says that in the wild, mothers lay their eggs near active volcanoes, to warm them until they hatch," Holly informed the others. "Apparently, it takes years."

"I could cast a spell to keep the eggs warm," Raven offered.

When Raven performed her spell, the Evil Queen secretly added power to it. The eggs got so hot that they began to hatch early!

Luckily, the baby dragons were a hit at Ever After High, and it was Holly and Poppy who took charge of caring for them.

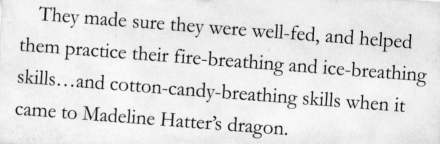

They made sure they were well-fed, and helped them practice their fire-breathing and ice-breathing skills…and cotton-candy-breathing skills when it came to Madeline Hatter's dragon.

The O'Hair twins were so dedicated to the baby dragons that one night they even accidentally fell asleep in the stables…and were woken up by a special surprise.

"Ew, dragon breath!" cried Poppy as a dragon licked her face. Holly giggled.

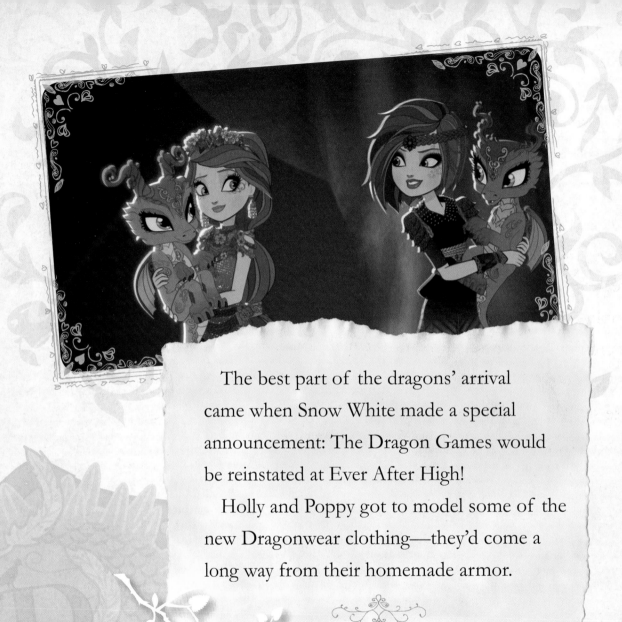

The best part of the dragons' arrival
came when Snow White made a special
announcement: The Dragon Games would
be reinstated at Ever After High!

Holly and Poppy got to model some of the
new Dragonwear clothing—they'd come a
long way from their homemade armor.

Snow White and the Evil Queen—who had finally revealed herself and promised to stop causing trouble—put on a dragon-riding demonstration for the crowd. Then it was time for the girls to take to the field with their baby dragons. Since the dragons were still too little to ride, Poppy and the others practiced training them instead.

At halftime, the teams brought their dragons back to the stables for some refreshments. What they didn't know, however, was that the Evil Queen wasn't keeping her promise. Faybelle Thorn had put a growth formula in the dragons' food.

By the time they got back out onto the field, their dragons were full-size—and the girls could ride them!

Their first official Dragon Games match ended in chaos, however, as the Evil Queen continued to show her true evil colors. She forced Nevermore to breathe fire on the school.

"She did it," Raven said to Nevermore, watching flames light up the campus. "She took control of the entire school!"

Raven knew she had to stop her mother—
and she needed the help of her friends and
their dragons.

Darling Charming led Raven, Holly, Poppy,
and the others to a secluded part of the
Enchanted Forest with their dragons. There,
they came up with a plan for Raven to lure
her mother out of the castle.

The Evil Queen may have been one of the greatest Dragon Games captains ever after, but she was no match for Raven and her best friends forever after.

"Noooooo!" she shrieked as Raven and Apple pulled her back into the mirror realm.

With the Evil Queen trapped again, Ever After High went back to normal. Well, almost normal—there were still dragons!

And no one was happier about that than Raven and Holly and Poppy O'Hair.